BunnyBear

ANDREA J. LONEY

pictures by
CARMEN SALDAÑA

ALBERT WHITMAN & COMPANY
CHICAGO, ILLINOIS

To my beloved family, old and new, near and far—AJL

To Angel, Roberta, Marcus, and Surimi—CS

Library of Congress Cataloging-in-Publication data is on file with the publisher.

Text copyright © 2017 by Andrea J. Loney
Pictures copyright © 2017 by Carmen Saldaña
Published in 2017 by Albert Whitman & Company
ISBN 978-0-8075-0938-8

Printed in China
10 9 8 7 6 5 4 3 2 1 LP 20 19 18 17 16

Design by Jordan Kost

For more information about Albert Whitman & Company,
visit our web site at www.albertwhitman.com.

There once was a bear who
was more than a bear.

Sure, he was shaggy and stompy like most bears. And he could be loud—very loud—if he wanted to.

But when he was alone, he loved to bounce through the forest, wiggle his nose, and nibble on strawberries. It made him feel free and light and happy.

He called himself Bunnybear.

The other bears didn't understand Bunnybear. They thought he was odd.
"WHAT ARE YOU DOING?" they growled.

So Bunnybear left the den
without even telling his mama.
He bounced through the forest
and into the meadow.

Then, right there in a patch of tasty flowers, he saw it! A bunny! He tried to say hello, but the rabbit raced away. Bunnybear bounce-bounce-bounced after her.

Underground, Bunnybear saw the most beautiful sight—an entire warren of bunnies. They were tiny and fluffy and bouncy, like Bunnybear's heart.

"What are you doing in here?" whispered one of the bunnies. Bunny whispers were one of Bunnybear's favorite sounds.

"Me? I'm just one of the bunnies," Bunnybear replied, a little too loudly.

The bunnies giggled. Bunny giggles were also one of Bunnybear's favorite sounds but not when the giggles were about him. They made Bunnybear feel cramped and fidgety.

The elder bunny looked down his long nose at Bunnybear. "You don't look like a bunny. You don't sound like a bunny. And"—he sniffed—"you certainly don't smell like a bunny."

"But," Bunnybear gasped. "I feel bouncy. And fluffy. And tiny. See?"

He wriggled his tail and bounced. But his bounces were a little too big.

"I think you should go,"
the elder bunny said.

All alone and covered with dirt, Bunnybear curled up against a tree and sighed. He didn't feel like a bear. He didn't look like a bunny. What was Bunnybear to do?

Then he felt a poke on his paw.
When he looked down, he saw a
bunny. Only this bunny was more
than a bunny.

"I'M GRIZZLYBUN!" she roared.
"You're awfully loud for a bunny," said Bunnybear.
"I'M NO BUNNY," said Grizzlybun. "I'M A BEAR!"

Nose to nose with Grizzlybun, Bunnybear asked, "Are you sure you're a bear?"

"OF COURSE I AM!" said Grizzlybun.
"I'M BURLY AND LOUD AND I EAT
WHATEVER I WANT!"

"That certainly sounds like a bear
to me," said Bunnybear.

"Really?" whispered Grizzlybun. "I mean, REALLY?"

"Yes," said Bunnybear. "You just look one way on the outside and feel another way on the inside. That's okay."

"I'M SURE GLAD YOU'RE HERE,"
said Grizzlybun.
   "Really? But I scared
everyone away."

"NOT ME," said Grizzlybun. "WHEN I SEE YOU, I FEEL MORE LIKE ME."

Grizzlybun's words made Bunnybear's heart bounce with joy. He gave her the biggest, bunniest bear hug ever.

So Bunnybear and Grizzlybun
found the perfect place to be
themselves. They played and giggled
and roared with laughter.

And they weren't just bunnies or bears. They were friends and they were happy. Until...

"WHERE HAVE YOU BEEN?" growled Mama Bear.

"I found a new friend, Mama! And she likes me just the way I am."
His mother gave him the biggest, coziest Mama Bear hug ever.
"I'm so happy for you, my sweet Bunnybear," she said in a beary whisper.

"Well done, my ferocious Grizzlybun,"
the elder bunny said. "Let's go home."

The next day, the bunnies threw a party and all the animals in the forest were invited.

Finally Bunnybear felt like he belonged.